YOU BE
THE JURY

YOU BE
THE JURY

Marvin Miller

Illustrated by Bob Roper

SCHOLASTIC INC.
New York Toronto London Auckland Sydney

All names used in this book are fictional, and any resemblance to any person living or dead is purely coincidental.

ISBN 0-590-40193-9

12 11 10 9   0 1 2/9

Printed in the U.S.A.   42

First Scholastic printing, October 1987

. .for Robby. . . . .

CONTENTS

Order in the Court

LADIES AND GENTLEMEN OF THE JURY:
This court is now in session. My name is Judge John Denenberg. You are the jury, and the trials are set to begin.

You have a serious responsibility. Will the innocent be sent to jail and the guilty go free? Let's hope not. Your job is to make sure that justice is served.

Read each case carefully. Study the evidence presented and then decide:

INNOCENT OR GUILTY??

Both sides of the case will be presented to you. The person who has the complaint is called the *plaintiff*. He has brought the case to court.

The person being accused is called the *defend-*

1

ant. He is pleading his innocence and presents a much different version of what happened.

IN EACH CASE, THREE PIECES OF EVIDENCE WILL BE PRESENTED AS EXHIBITS A, B, AND C. EXAMINE THE EXHIBITS VERY CAREFULLY. A *CLUE* TO THE SOLUTION OF EACH CASE WILL BE FOUND THERE. IT WILL DIRECTLY POINT TO THE INNOCENCE OR GUILT OF THE ACCUSED.

Remember, each side will try to convince you that his version is what actually happened. BUT YOU MUST MAKE THE FINAL DECISION.

The Case of
the Dangerous Golf Ball

LADIES AND GENTLEMEN OF THE JURY:
If you are hit on the head by a golf ball while playing golf, there is very little that you can do legally. When you set foot on a golf course, you accept the risks that may occur. However, if you are standing in your house and are hit on the head by a golf ball, that is quite a different matter.

Such is the case before you today. Jason Compson, the plaintiff, is one of the homeowners of Green Acres Homes. He is suing the developer because a stray golf ball hit him while he was inside his house. Green Acres Development Corporation, the defendant, claims that Mr. Compson's injury is a complete fabrication, designed to harass them.

Mr. Compson has testified as follows:

"My name is Jason Compson. Two years ago, I bought one of the first homes in the Green Acres Housing Development. My home is one of sixty homes surrounding a private nine-hole golf course. Home buyers were invited to join the golf club, which was to be a private recreation center for the housing development."

During its first year, very few people joined the golf club. The club realized it would have to go out of business unless more people joined, so it announced it would change its policies and open the club to the general public.

To accommodate its plans, the club added an additional nine holes, clearing the trees near Mr. Compson's property.

Mr. Compson was upset. When he had purchased his home, he could sit on the patio overlooking the wooded land, barely seeing the golf course in the distance. When the new course was built, trees had been cleared, and he could now see the sixth tee which was fifty yards from his patio.

Before building the new course, Green Acres assured Mr. Compson it would be designed so that all golf shots would point away from his property. But it said nothing about the view. Besides seeing the sixth hole from his patio, Mr. Compson complained that when his windows were open, the constant chatter of golfers could be heard in his house.

Mr. Compson was so angry that he tried to get Green Acres to move the sixth tee. Mr. Compson claimed that the noise of the golfers calling, "caddy!" caused him mental distress, and he was in danger of bodily harm from a stray golf ball.

One day, Mr. Compson's prediction came true.

As he was in his den, hanging an expensive mirror, a golf ball shot through the window, hitting him on the head. He lost his grip and the mirror crashed on the mantle and fell to the floor.

Besides his injury, the mirror was completely shattered. The mantle was also heavily damaged.

Mr. Compson has sued Green Acres for his pain and suffering and for the cost to replace the broken mirror and repair the mantle. He further claims that the accident is proof of the unsafe location of the sixth tee and demands that Green Acres rebuild it farther away from his house.

EXHIBIT A shows the inside of Mr. Compson's den and the broken mirror. From the broken window, you can note the path the ball took directly across from where the mirror was being hung.

EXHIBIT B is a photograph of Mr. Compson, taken two days after the accident. Mr. Compson's lawyer asks you to note the large bandage and dark circles around his eyes. His injury took more than two weeks to heal.

The management of Green Acres presents a different view of the case. They claim that it was impossible for the accident to have occurred. They also state that Compson has repeatedly threatened the management.

A vice-president for Green Acres has testified: "I don't need any photographs or EXHIBIT B's to recognize Compson. I'd know him anywhere by his voice. At least once a day ever since the new course was built, Compson has been telephoning our office complaining about the noise. Compson also complained he would occasionally see a golfer in his backyard, looking for a stray ball and trespassing on his property."

Green Acres posted a guard near Compson's home but was never able to confirm Compson's complaints.

Green Acres argues that Mr. Compson's complaining was staged for the sole purpose of bothering the club. Green Acres offers as proof EXHIBIT C, showing the location of the sixth tee in relation to Compson's house. Because of the direction of the hole, it would be highly unlikely for a golfer to drive the ball into Mr. Compson's window.

Green Acres further claims that Compson had purposely faked the accident, and broke the mirror and mantle himself. They claim that Compson had no witness to the accident.

Green Acres requests the Court to dismiss Compson's charges, and asks that he be stopped from bothering the club and its golfers.

LADIES AND GENTLEMEN OF THE JURY: You have just heard the Case of the Dangerous Golf Ball. You must decide the merit of Jason Compson's claim. Be sure to carefully examine the evidence in EXHIBITS A, B, and C.

Could a golfer on the sixth tee have accidentally driven a ball through Jason Compson's window? Or did he stage the accident to dramatize his unhappiness with the new golf course?

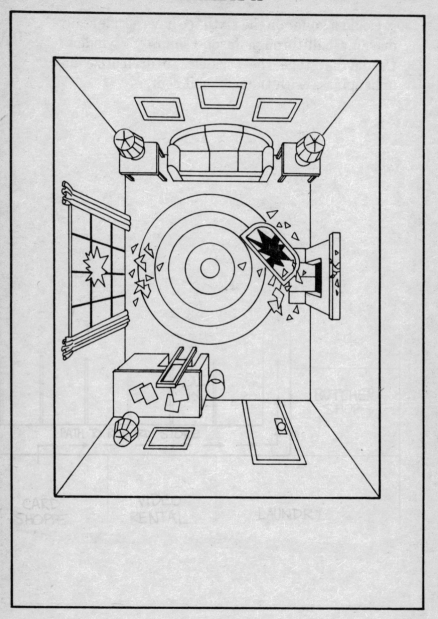

EXHIBIT C

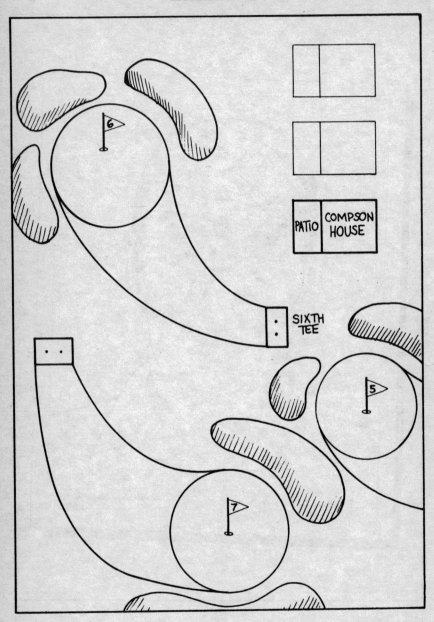

10

The Case of
The Rotten Apples

LADIES AND GENTLEMEN OF THE JURY:
A person does not have the legal right to commit a criminal act while defending his own private property.

That is the point of law you must keep in mind today. Arthur Hallow, the plaintiff, admits that he trespassed on the farm property of Farmer Frost, the defendant. But Mr. Hallow charges that when he did so, he was viciously attacked by Mr. Frost, and that Frost broke Hallow's arm. Arthur Hallow is suing Farmer Frost for assault, and is asking for money to pay his medical bills. Farmer Frost says that Arthur Hallow is lying.

Arthur Hallow has testified to the following:

"On the evening of October 5, around six o'clock, I was hiking along Somerset Road. I passed the woods that mark the start of Farmer Frost's property. I know Farmer Frost lives there, but there's no sign or anything that says to keep out.

"Along the edge of the woods is a path leading to the Frost farmhouse. I started down the path because it also leads to the Frost orchard. Everyone knows Farmer Frost has the best apples around. I planned to fill my knapsack with apples. I've done it lots of times before and nothing ever happened."

After Hallow reached the orchard, he leaned against a tree to rest. Suddenly he yelled out loud. He had backed up against a patched tree and could feel the wet tar seeping through his shirt.

I refer again to the actual testimony of Arthur Hallow when questioned by his attorney. First the question and then the answer:

Q What happened after you yelled?

A I started picking apples from the ground and filling my knapsack. Most of the apples on the ground were rotten.

Q Did you climb any of the trees?

A I was about to when I heard a voice behind me. It was Old Frosty, and he shouted for me to stop.

Q What was the name you just used?

A Old Frosty. That's what everyone calls Farmer Frost because he's so mean and has a nasty temper.

Q Then what happened?

A I turned around and saw he was pointing a gun at me. I was frightened and promised I would give him back his apples.

Q What was his reply?

A He was upset. He put down his gun and attacked me. I tried to run, but he grabbed me from behind in a bear hug. I dropped the apples. He grabbed my left wrist and twisted it behind my back.

Q Did you attempt to defend yourself?

A No. I cried for him to stop. He was hurting my arm. The more I yelled, the more he pulled. Suddenly my arm went limp and a sharp pain shot through it.

Q When did Frost let go?

A When he realized what he had done, he backed away and picked up his rifle. He kept it pointed at me until the police arrived.

Arthur Hallow was rushed to the local hospital where X-rays revealed a broken arm. He wants Farmer Frost to pay for the medical bills.

Farmer Frost presents a completely different explanation of what happened. First of all, he states that his property is indeed marked. EXHIBIT A is the "No Trespassing" sign found by the police near the path leading to Farmer Frost's house. The police have said it was clearly visible from Somerset Road.

In addition, Farmer Frost has made the following statement:

"I was just sitting down to dinner when I heard a loud cry from out in the orchard. It sounded like someone was hurt, so I immediately called the police."

EXHIBIT B is the police record of this call.

As he waited for the police, Frost heard another yell followed by a thud. He peered out the window and saw Arthur Hallow slowly picking himself up from the ground. Presumably he had fallen from a tree. The youth held his arm and began running toward Somerset Road.

Frost took his gun and ran after the trespasser. He quickly caught up with him and held him at gunpoint. Moments later, the police arrived. EXHIBIT C is a photograph taken at the scene.

Farmer Frost claims he had nothing to do with Arthur Hallow's broken arm, and he refuses to pay the medical expenses.

LADIES AND GENTLEMEN OF THE JURY: You have just heard the Case of the Rotten Apples. You must decide the merit of Arthur Hallow's claim. Be sure to carefully examine the evidence in EXHIBITS A, B, and C.

Is Farmer Frost guilty of the assault as charged? Or did Arthur Hallow make up the entire story?

D.D. 5

CRIME CLASSIFICATION	POLICE DEPARTMENT REPORT
TRESPASSING	

NAME OF COMPLAINANT	ADDRESS
FARMER FROST	5 Somerset Road

6:40 P.M. phone call. Complainant heard noise outside his house on the grounds of his apple grove. Believes he heard someone yelling.

Dispatched Car 43 to location.

Greg Baldwin
OFFICER ON DUTY

EXHIBIT C

The Case of
The Squashed Scooter

LADIES AND GENTLEMEN OF THE JURY:
If the driver of a car accidentally damages
another vehicle that is improperly parked, the
driver is not responsible for any damage.

While Archy Leaf, the plaintiff, was shopping
at Cherry Hill Mall, his motor scooter was run
over by a car driven by Butch Brando, the
defendant. Mr. Leaf charges that Mr. Brando
purposely ran over the scooter to get even with
him. Butch Brando says he is not responsible for
the accident and will not pay for the damages.

Archy Leaf has given the following testimony:
"It was Saturday afternoon, July 24. I rode my
motor scooter over to the Cherry Hill Mall and
parked in an empty parking space. I stopped in
at the Card Shoppe for a birthday card for my
girl friend. Then I went into Rush Records. My
favorite group, Engine Summer, had a new tape
out, and I wanted to see if the store had it.

"I remember passing my motor scooter on the
way to Rush Records. It was parked upright."

Leaf was in the record store for about five

minutes when he heard a loud crunch and ran outside. To his horror, he saw his scooter lying crushed under the wheels of Butch Brando's car. Several shoppers gathered around the accident, but there were no eyewitnesses.

EXHIBIT A is a map of Cherry Hill Mall with the path Archy Leaf took from the card store to the record shop.

EXHIBIT B is a photograph of the accident scene. You will note the scooter's tangled wreckage under the car.

Archy Leaf continued with his testimony:

"My scooter was properly parked, I'm sure of that. But more important, this was no accident, I can tell you. Butch Brando was out to get me. He's been mad at me for the past two weeks. We both have summer jobs working at Burger Palace. Butch has been coming back from lunch later and later every day, and I finally had to tell the boss. There's too much work for me to handle all by myself.

"The day after I spoke with the boss, Butch came up to me in the parking lot. 'You won't get away with this,' he said. 'I'll get even no matter what. Just wait and see. You'll be *shaking* like a leaf, Leaf, before I'm through with you.' I'm sure Butch Brando ran over my scooter on purpose."

Mr. Leaf seeks payment for damages of $280.00.

Butch Brando has presented a very different version of what happened. I will now read from his testimony. First the question from his attorney and then Mr. Brando's answer:

Q Where were you on the afternoon of Saturday, July 24?

A I was driving around in my car. I love my car. There's no way I would ever do anything that might put a dent in it.

Q When you drove into the mall, what did you see?

A The parking lot was crowded with cars. There were a few motorcycles and scooters parked, but I didn't see Archy's scooter anywhere, if that's what you mean. I finally found a narrow parking space between a van and another car. The van was hogging part of the space.

Q Did you see a motor scooter in that space?

A I certainly did not. At least not from my view behind the wheel. The front of my car sticks out pretty far.

Q Then what happened?

A I drove slowly into the space. All of a sudden I heard something crunch under the wheels of my car. I immediately put on the brakes.

Q How long have you known Archy Leaf?

A Archy and I are old friends. We used to be in Mrs. Kowalski's class back in grade school. He's kind of a nervous little guy, you know what I mean? So I like to tease him, but he knows I'm only kidding. I'd never do anything to hurt him.

22

Mr. Brando further stated that when he drove his car into the parking space he saw two young boys running away from the scene. He suggests that if the scooter was not carelessly parked flat on the ground by Leaf himself, then the two boys may have knocked it down.

Witnesses have stated that there *were* vandals at the mall at the time, spraying shaving cream across the windows of several cars. Brando offers as proof EXHIBIT C, which is a police complaint by a shopper whose window was sprayed by vandals around the time of this accident.

Butch Brando says that the scooter was lying *flat* on the parking space ground. Since it was parked improperly he was unable to see it. Mr. Brando requests the charges against him be dismissed because the accident was due to Leaf's own carelessness.

LADIES AND GENTLEMEN OF THE JURY: You have just heard the Case of the Squashed Scooter. You must decide the merit of Mr. Leaf's claim. Be sure to carefully examine the evidence in EXHIBITS A, B, and C.

Did Butch Brando knowingly drive his car over Archy Leaf's motor scooter? Or was it an accident?

EXHIBIT A

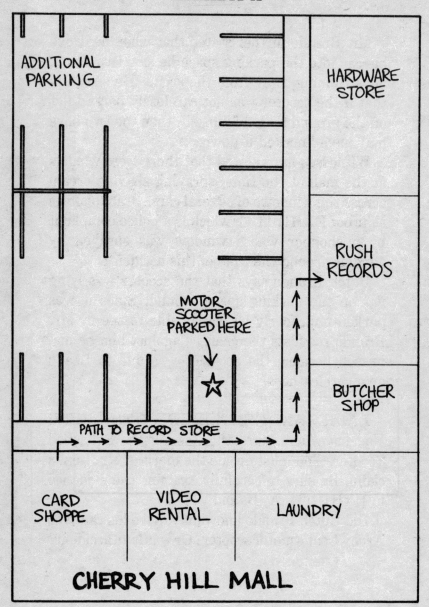

EXHIBIT C

CRIME CLASSIFICATION	POLICE DEPARTMENT REPORT
VANDALISM	

NAME OF COMPLAINANT	ADDRESS
MS. SANDRA HELFANO	844 Wingate Terrace

11:17 A.M. Complainant was shopping inside Green's Hardware Store. Claims that two young boys were creating a disturbance in the parking lot of the Cherry Hill Mall. She saw them spraying shaving cream across the windows of cars.

Greg Baldwin

OFFICER ON DUTY

VERDICT

BRANDO SQUASHED
THE SCOOTER ON PURPOSE.

The motor scooter, shown in EXHIBIT B, was crushed under the *rear* wheels of Butch Brando's car. If, as Brando had claimed in his testimony, he stopped the car immediately when he heard the crunch, the motor scooter would have been under the *front* wheels. Brando purposely ran over Leaf's scooter.

The Case of
The Wrong Bag

LADIES AND GENTLEMEN OF THE JURY:
A person who is found with stolen property is
not necessarily a thief.

Keep this in mind as you go over the facts in
this case. Since we are in criminal court today,
the State is the accuser. In this case, the State,
represented by the district attorney, has accused
John Summers of robbing Kay's Jewelry Store.
John Summers, the defendant, has pleaded innocent and claims that his arrest is a mistake.

The State called the owner of Kay's Jewelry
Store as its first witness. She has testified as
follows:

"My name is Wendy Kay, and I own Kay's
Jewelry Store in Martinville. I was working alone
in the store on Wednesday afternoon, December
2, when a man walked in. It was exactly 3:30. I
noticed the time because I had just put a new
collection of diamond watches from Switzerland
on display. I noticed the man because he had a
handkerchief over his face. I thought that was
odd until I also noticed the outline of a gun

projecting from his pocket. That's when I got scared."

The man ordered Wendy Kay to empty a case of jewels and all the store's cash into a black bag. The robbery took only minutes, and the thief escaped on foot.

At four o'clock the next afternoon, John Summers entered the lobby of the Bristol Hotel and walked over to the luggage checkroom. He pointed to a black bag, which the bellman gave him. As he handed the bellman a tip, a hotel detective noticed that Summers' bag matched the description of the bag used in the jewelry store robbery. He arrested Summers and called the police.

When the police opened the bag and emptied its contents, a look of shock and surprise spread over Summer's face. Inside was the stolen jewelry.

John Summers was dumbfounded. He claimed he had pointed to the wrong bag in the hotel checkroom. This bag was not his, he said, but an identical twin belonging to someone else. His own bag contained a blue toothbrush and underwear, and it was locked.

The police returned to the luggage checkroom and questioned the bellman. The man thought there might have been two bags in the checkroom, although a second black bag was nowhere to be found.

EXHIBIT A is a picture of the bag and jewelry.

John Summers claims that he checked an identical bag and that he mistakenly picked up this bag from the luggage room.

The State has drawn your attention to the shape of this bag, its handle, and lock. The State submits that this is an unusual-looking bag, and that it is very unlikely, if not impossible, that another bag looking just like it would be checked into the same hotel on the same day.

The State also presented EXHIBIT B, a list of the contents of John Summers' pockets at the time he was arrested. His wallet contained $710 in cash, a sizable sum for a person spending only one night in town. The State alleges that the $710 in Summers' wallet is the money stolen from the jewelry store.

No gun was found in Summers' pocket. The State claims a simple explanation. John Summers robbed Kay's Jewelry Store by pretending the object in his pocket was a gun. In reality, it was only his pointed finger.

On the basis of all this evidence, John Summers was accused of the jewelry store robbery.

John Summers has given the following testimony:

"My visit to Martinville was supposed to be a simple overnight trip. Every year around this time, the Martinville Museum has its annual art sale, and I wanted to buy a painting. I just started collecting art last year. I may not know a lot about art, but I know what I like. I've already got two of those pictures of the sad-looking kids with the big eyes. But this time I wanted something really stupendous to go over the sofa in the living room. Maybe something with some purple in it to match the drapes. I saved up more than eight hundred bucks to buy a painting this trip."

Summers' schedule was easy to reconstruct. He arrived by bus on Wednesday morning and checked into the Bristol Hotel. The Museum opened at noon. Mr. Summers was one of the first persons to enter the Museum. He spent the entire afternoon there. But to his disappointment, he could not find any artwork he liked.

EXHIBIT C is a torn Museum ticket stub for the day in question. The Museum hours were noon to four o'clock. The robbery of Kay's Jewelry Store took place at 3:30. While there was no witness who can testify he saw John Summers in the Museum the entire time, the stub shows he indeed visited the Museum.

When the Museum closed, John Summers went back to his hotel, disappointed his trip was in vain. The following day, he checked out of the hotel at noon. Since his bus did not leave until later that day, Summers locked his black bag, checked it in the hotel's luggage checkroom, and went sightseeing. Later he returned to pick up his bag, and he was promptly arrested.

John Summers claims that he is the victim of

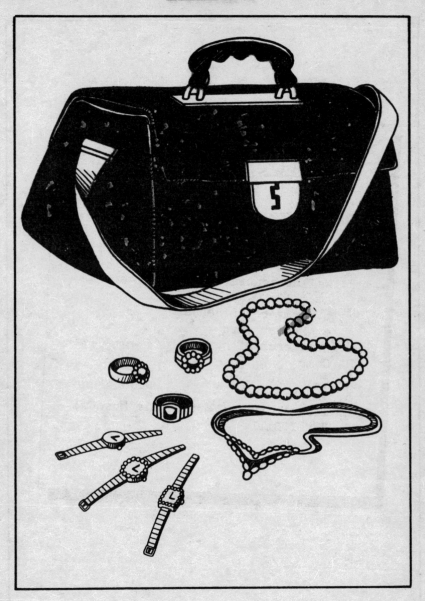

POLICE ⬟PD⬟ DEPARTMENT

JOHN SUMMERS

Contents of pockets

1. Wallet contents:
   a. $710.00 cash
   b. Driver's License
   c. Master Card
2. Handkerchief
3. Comb
4. $1.25 in coins
5. Chewing Gum
6. Ticket Stub (Martinville Museum)
7. Hotel Bill

EXHIBIT C

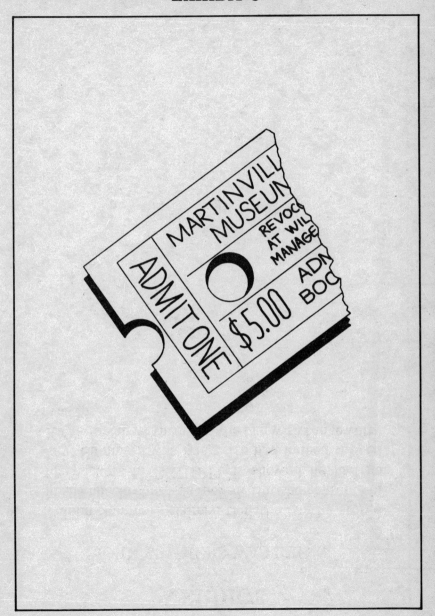

VERDICT

JOHN SUMMERS WAS LYING.

John Summers claimed that the bag he stored in the checkroom was *locked*. But the contents of his pockets in EXHIBIT B showed he had no key. Summers was lying. He had indeed robbed Kay's Jewelry Store, and the bag with the jewelry was his.

The Case of
the Missing Will

LADIES AND GENTLEMEN OF THE JURY:
People write wills so that when they die their wealth can be passed along according to their instructions. A person may change his or her will as many times as he or she likes. However, it is the last will that is considered to be legal.

Stanley Woot was a wealthy businessman and inventor. He had two children, Barbara and Stan, Jr. When he died last July, his will revealed that he had left all his money to his daughter Barbara. Stan, Jr. has contested this will. Stan, Jr. claims that he has discovered a later will which states that he and Barbara should share their father's money equally.

Barbara Woot has given the following testimony:

"As you all know, my father was very successful all his life. He made his first fortune at the age of nineteen by inventing the little metal band that holds the eraser onto the end of a pencil. The only unsuccessful part of his life was his personal life. I'm speaking about my younger brother, Stan, Jr.

"Stan, Jr. was always a problem child. As he grew older, he would do anything to avoid work. He seemed to think that life was one big party. It always hurt me to see how unhappy he made my father."

The relationship between father and son grew strained, and five years ago Stanley Woot cut off all financial support. Stan, Jr. then moved to another part of the state, and the two rarely saw each other.

In July, Stanley Woot died following a long illness. The following day, the family's lawyer met the children in the library of the Woot mansion for the reading of the will. In it, Stanley Woot had left his entire fortune to his daughter Barbara.

Stan, Jr. protested. He claimed that a week before his father's death, his father contacted him. The elder Woot knew his illness was serious and proposed they reestablish their relationship. In return, Stan, Jr. promised he would change his idle ways. The elder Woot then drafted a new will.

Barbara was skeptical when she heard this story. But Stan, Jr. sought to prove that a newer will existed.

The evening following the reading of the will, Stan, Jr. searched through his father's house. By morning he had discovered an envelope containing a *new* will in his father's desk drawer. The new will stated that Stan, Jr. and Barbara should share their father's fortune equally.

Barbara Woot testified further:

"Stan, Jr. says he has changed his ways, but he has not. In fact, just before our father's death, Stan, Jr. flew to Paris for the weekend and went on a shopping spree. He charged everything to Dad's account."

When Stanley Woot received the bills, he became so angry that he immediately published a notice in newspapers around the world. The official notice, which disavows responsibility for his son's actions, appeared just two weeks before Stanley Woot died. This notice is EXHIBIT A.

Barbara Woot says that Stan, Jr. is lying: There was no change in his relationship with his father, and the will he claims to have discovered is a fake.

Stan, Jr. has testified as follows:

"It's true, my father and I were never close. Ever since I can remember, we've argued about something, mostly money and my friends. Maybe if he hadn't been so wrapped up in his business, things would have been different. . . .

"The week before he died, my father called me. He had been sick for a long time and knew he didn't have much time left. He told me he wanted us to work out our problems, he was sorry he'd failed as a father, and he asked me to forgive him."

Stan, Jr. says that he visited his father, not once but several times during the last week of Stanley Woot's life. Testimony of the family housekeeper, which is entered as EXHIBIT B, is offered as proof that father and son were again on good terms.

Although she did not overhear their actual conversations, the housekeeper could detect no sign of anger between them. In contrast, the housekeeper stated that in earlier years, Stan, Jr. and his father quarreled bitterly — and loudly.

Stan, Jr. has told the court:

"You've heard that my father and I finally mended our relationship. Naturally, I was shocked when the will was read and in it my father left everything to my sister Barbara. Since my father had told me he was making out a new will, I thought maybe he hadn't had a chance to give it to his attorney. I decided to see if I could find the new will at his house. The next morning, while I was searching through his desk, I found the envelope containing the new will. As you can see, my father has asked that his estate be divided equally between Barbara and me."

EXHIBIT C is the new will itself.

LADIES AND GENTLEMEN OF THE JURY: You have just heard the Case of the Missing Will. You must decide the merit of Stan, Jr.'s claim.

Be sure to carefully examine the evidence in EXHIBITS A, B, and C.

Is the will found by Stan, Jr. the last will and testament of Stanley Woot? Or is it a fake?

EXHIBIT A

ANNOUNCEMENTS

BE A MILLIONAIRE
New easy method.
Works while you sleep.
Call 355-1212 after midnight.

**STOP SMOKING
LOSE WEIGHT
See results fast.
"IT'S ALL DONE
WITH MIRRORS"
For more information call
976-5858**

I, Stanley Woot,
will not be responsible
for any debts of Stan Woot, Jr.

**MUSIC 'N THINGS
THE FUN HOME PARTY
Sell band instruments**

EXHIBIT B

STATEMENT OF GRETA BURROWS

I have been the housekeeper for the late Stanley Woot for fourteen years. During this period, I have been in the house several times when he was visited by his son, Stan Jr.

The relationship between father and son was not very friendly. Over the past several years, whenever the two met, their talks always ended in Stanley Woot yelling at his son and his son yelling back. Each time, Stanley Woot accused his son of being lazy with no ambition to make anything of himself. Each meeting ended with Stan Jr. leaving the house in tears and Mr. Woot telling his son never to come back.

But several times a year, months after their fight, Stanley Woot would telephone his son and ask him to come to the house again. When he did, the fighting would soon start.

During the week preceding the death of Stanley Woot, he again called his son. When Stan Jr. came to the house, it was the first time I was there that the two of them did not have a bitter argument. They met for an hour behind the closed door of Stanley Woot's den. I did not overhear the conversation, but I can state that they definitely did not yell at one another.

During the final week, there was nothing I saw or heard that would lead me to believe they were angry with one another.

(signed) Greta Burrows

(notarized)

sworn to me this 21 day of
July, 1985.

EXHIBIT C

July 7, 1985

To whom it may concern;

    This is my last will. I give and bequeath to my daughter Barbara Woot and my son Stan Woot Jr., to be

divided equally, in complete and perfect ownership, all my rights and property of every kind and nature, whether real or personal.

Stanley Woot

VERDICT

THE NEW WILL IS A FAKE.

The will that was found by Stan, Jr. in EX-HIBIT C is folded once. But it is too large to fit into the envelope. Stan, Jr. had typed the will, forged his father's signature, grabbed an envelope, and brought them to the lawyer. But he neglected to make sure the will fit inside the envelope.

The Case of
the Fast Getaway

LADIES AND GENTLEMEN OF THE JURY:
Just because a man has been found guilty of a crime once before, this does not mean he will be a criminal forever.

The State, represented by the district attorney, has accused Frank Carson of robbing Party Poopers, Inc. Frank Carson, the defendant, says that he is innocent.

The State called Glinda Harris as its first witness:

"My name is Glinda Harris. I'm the office manager of Party Poopers, Inc. We make and sell all kinds of party supplies and novelties. You know those little bottles that pop and shoot out confetti when you pull the string? Those are our party poppers. Our most famous item is our Party Pooper whoopee cushion. We've sold nearly a million this year alone.

"On Friday morning, October 28, I arrived at our office on the fifth floor of Glendale Plaza at eight o'clock. I like to get to work early so I can prepare the office for the day.

"As I was opening the office safe there was a knock on the back door. I thought it was an employee who had forgotten their key, so I opened the door."

Glinda Harris was confronted by a man, about six feet tall, wearing a bulky blue down jacket, and holding a knife. A yellow paper party hat was pulled down over part of his face.

The intruder grabbed Glinda Harris from behind. Warning her not to scream, he dragged her over to an exposed water pipe and chained her left arm to it. The robber emptied the safe of $2,000 in cash, stuffing it into a paper trick-or-treat bag he was carrying. He threw down the knife and fled, escaping in a green and white sports car.

The police later found that the realistic-looking knife was actually made out of rubber.

The following day, a man identified as Frank Carson was stopped while traveling 60 miles per hour in a 35 mile zone. His facial features, clothes, and car were similar to those described by Glinda Harris. EXHIBIT A is a copy of the burglar's description which Glinda Harris gave to the police.

Based on this description, Frank Carson was placed under arrest. When Carson was arrested, the police found eight hundred dollars in cash hidden in his left shoe. They also found a notice in his car that he owed his bank $1,000. The State contends that it seems suspicious that Carson would be carrying $800 in cash while being unable to pay the $1,000 bank loan. The State argues that the cash in Carson's shoe was from the robbery.

Further investigation by the police turned up the fact that Frank Carson had been arrested before. EXHIBIT B is information taken from Frank Carson's permanent criminal record. The State has asked you to note the similarity between these earlier crimes and the robbery at Party Poopers. Based on all this evidence, the State asks that you find Frank Carson guilty as charged.

Frank Carson says that he is innocent. He has testified as follows:

"Yes, it's true. I used to be a bad character. But that was a long time ago. Since then I've gone straight. These days I'm a consultant for the TV networks. You may wonder what experience I have that would interest a TV company. Well, whenever they're doing a crime show, they call on me — to make sure all the crimes look realistic."

Frank Carson's lawyer has also challenged the description by Glinda Harris that led to the arrest. He claims that the information she gave was too general to prove that Frank Carson was the robber. Many people could fit the description given by Mrs. Harris. To further cast doubt on the description, Frank Carson's lawyer has presented

EXHIBIT C, a diagram of the room where the robbery was committed.

You will note that the safe is on the opposite side of the room from the water pipe where Glinda Harris was chained. Thus the robber probably had his back to Mrs. Harris most of the time he was in the room.

Because of the weaknesses in Glinda Harris' case, Frank Carson asks that the charges be dropped.

LADIES AND GENTLEMEN OF THE JURY: You have just heard the Case of the Fast Getaway. You must decide the merits of the State's accusation. Be sure to carefully examine the evidence in EXHIBITS A, B, and C.

Is Frank Carson guilty of robbing Party Poopers, Inc.? Or was the robbery committed by someone else?

EXHIBIT A

D.D.5

CRIME CLASSIFICATION	POLICE DEPARTMENT REPORT
ROBBERY	

NAME OF COMPLAINANT	ADDRESS
GLINDA HARRIS	42 Glendale Plaza

Be on the lookout for suspect wanted in connection with robbery at Party Poopers, Inc.

Description:

    age: 25-35

    height: 6 feet

    hair: color unknown

    eyes: blue or green

    weight: heavy build

When last seen was wearing: blue down jacket, blue jeans, running shoes.

Escaped in green and white two-door sports car.

Make and model unknown.

Greg Baldwin

OFFICER ON DUTY

EXHIBIT B

INFORMATION FROM CRIMINAL RECORD

Frank Carson

This man twice convicted on larceny and conspiracy to commit larceny on several counts.

$1,000 stolen from Greenbatch Supply Company, NYC at knifepoint on March 12, 1972.

Suspended sentence.

$5,000 stolen at knifepoint from Willis Knitting Factory, Ontego, NY May 20, 1974.

Served two years at Bradford NY prison.

No record of additional arrests.

EXHIBIT C

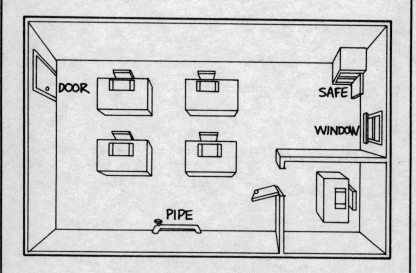

5TH FLOOR OFFICE
PARTY POOPERS, INC.

The Case of
the Power Blackout

LADIES AND GENTLEMEN OF THE JURY:
A company that provides a public service, such as a power company, has special responsibilities. When the service fails, the company is responsible for any damages that may happen.

Keep this in mind as you decide the case before you today. Mel Mudd, the plaintiff and owner of Mudd's Diner, claims that a power failure lasted sixteen hours and he was unable to serve his customers. Mr. Mudd wants to be paid for this lost business. Allied Utilities, the defendant, is a power company that provides electricity and gas to the people in Fairchester County. Allied Utilities admits to the power failure. But it claims to have repaired it three hours after it was reported.

Mel Mudd has given the following testimony:

"My name is Mudd. I'm the owner of Mudd's Diner. On Thursday, February 16 at 9:30 P.M., just as I was about to close up for the night, the lights went out. Do you know that old joke: Where was Thomas Edison when the lights went out? Well, the answer is: In the dark. And that's

The Case of
the Power Blackout

LADIES AND GENTLEMEN OF THE JURY:
A company that provides a public service, such as a power company, has special responsibilities. When the service fails, the company is responsible for any damages that may happen.

Keep this in mind as you decide the case before you today. Mel Mudd, the plaintiff and owner of Mudd's Diner, claims that a power failure lasted sixteen hours and he was unable to serve his customers. Mr. Mudd wants to be paid for this lost business. Allied Utilities, the defendant, is a power company that provides electricity and gas to the people in Fairchester County. Allied Utilities admits to the power failure. But it claims to have repaired it three hours after it was reported.

Mel Mudd has given the following testimony:

"My name is Mudd. I'm the owner of Mudd's Diner. On Thursday, February 16 at 9:30 P.M., just as I was about to close up for the night, the lights went out. Do you know that old joke: Where was Thomas Edison when the lights went out? Well, the answer is: In the dark. And that's exactly where I was, too. I immediately called the power company and was assured the power would be restored promptly."

Mr. Mudd returned to his diner the following morning, opened the back door and flipped on the light switch. The room was totally dark.

He telephoned the power company several times, and each time the line was busy. After posting a "closed" sign on the front of the diner, Mudd returned to the back room and tried to telephone the company again. The line was still busy.

Mr. Mudd kept phoning the utility company and after two hours finally got through. The company told him they had fixed the problem the night before, but they promised they would send a repairman right away.

It took two hours for the repairman to arrive. By that time, Mr. Mudd had turned away the noon lunch crowd.

The repairman again checked the outside cable. He tightened the couplings but found nothing to indicate further repairs were needed. When the repairman went back to the diner to report his findings, the lights were on in the back room.

Mr. Mudd insisted the second visit was necessary to repair the lost power because the work had not been done properly the night before. He telephoned Allied Utilities and told them he planned to sue the company for lost business. A supervisor arrived at the diner in five minutes.

EXHIBIT A shows the lost business at Mudd's Diner during the time Mudd claims he had no power. You will note on that day he had only $146.35 in business. Entries for other days show he usually had up to $450.00 worth of business. This is the amount Mudd seeks from the utility company — $450.00.

Mel Mudd was extremely angry when the supervisor arrived at the back room of the diner. The man assured Mudd the power failure had been fixed the night before. Mudd strongly disagreed.

Allied Utilities enters as EXHIBIT B the repair work-order for the diner. This is a record kept for each customer complaint. You will note that the first call came in at 9:35 P.M. The repair order shows that the power failure lasted only three hours during the time the diner was closed. Power was claimed to have been restored by 12:36 A.M.

The company also enters EXHIBIT C, a photograph of the back room that was taken shortly after the supervisor arrived. You will note that the supervisor is holding up a light bulb. He had found it in a wastebasket in the diner's back room. Tests have shown this bulb is burned out and no longer in working order.

The company contends that while its repairman was outside checking the power the second time, Mudd somehow realized he may have been mistaken about the power failure. The light in the back room had failed to go on because of a burned out bulb. Mr. Mudd then replaced the bulb with a new one but said nothing to the company so he could sue them for lost business. Allied Utilities refuses to pay the money Mel Mudd has requested.

LADIES AND GENTLEMEN OF THE JURY: You have just heard the Case of the Power Blackout. You must decide the merit of Mel Mudd's claim. Be sure to carefully examine the evidence in EXHIBITS A, B, and C.

Should Allied Utilities pay Mr. Mudd for the income he lost during the power failure? Or did Mudd know that the power had been restored?

GROSS RECIEPTS
WEEK OF FEB. 12

DATE	BREAKFAST 6-11	LUNCH 11-5	DINNER 5-9	TOTAL
2/12	93.25	116.40	170.50	380.15
2/13	123.60	88.25	225.80	437.63
2/14	85.25	116.45	248.70	450.40
2/15	47.65	93.85	286.45	427.95
2/16	48.10	106.75	254.05	408.90
2/17	—	20.00	126.35	146.35
2/18	94.45	123.20	204.20	421.85

WEEKLY TOTAL – $2,694.10

EXHIBIT B

ALLIED ⚡UTILITIES
TELEPHONE LOG

DATE	TIME	NAME	ADDRESS	REPAIR MAN	DIS. TIME	COMP. TIME
2/16	7:12p	B. ROPER	186 CHEW ST.	8	7:30p	7:50p
2/16	7:29p	G. MORRISI	S. POINT ST.	17	8:10p	8:55p
2/16	8:17p	K. SPENGLER	294 8TH ST.	15	8:30p	9:58p
2/16	8:42p	B. SEATED	26 BLAIR AVE.	8	9:30p	10:15p
2/16	9:35p	M. MUDD	15 SOUTH ST.	17	10:43p	12:36p
2/16	9:55p	R. LEMON	7 W. POINT	9	10:55p	11:30p
2/16	10:30p	H. RUBIN	19 2ND AVE.	8	11:15p	11:35p
2/16	10:47p	D. CLARK	40 TOMS RD.	15	12:00p	12:20p

EXHIBIT C

VERDICT

MUDD KNEW
THE POWER HAD BEEN RESTORED.

EXHIBIT C shows the back room of Mudd's Diner after the supervisor arrived. An empty glass with ice cubes is on a table. If the electricity was out until shortly before the supervisor got there, it would have been impossible for Mudd to have used ice cubes in the drink. When Mudd realized he had ice, he knew the power had been restored the night before. This was confirmed when he replaced the burned-out light bulb. However, he had already turned away his lunchtime customers, so he said nothing to the supervisor so he could illegally sue the power company.

The Case of The Speedy Jewel Thieves

LADIES AND GENTLEMEN OF THE JURY:

Whenever a theft occurs, a question logically arises. Did the person who was robbed fake the robbery in order to collect the insurance money?

That is the question presented to you today. Earl Rogers, the plaintiff, claims he was the victim of a robbery. Bowen Insurance Company, the defendant, refuses to pay the plaintiff's robbery claim. The insurance company's attorney states that there is not sufficient evidence to show that a robbery actually occurred.

Mr. Rogers has given the following testimony:

"On Sunday, June 20, at four o'clock in the afternoon, I was in my bedroom reading a book. The book was *Crime and Punishment*, to be exact. Deciding to take a nap, I lowered the shades and darkened the room. I was just drifting off to sleep when I heard strange noises coming from the den next to my bedroom."

Mr. Rogers put his ear to the bedroom door and strained to hear what was going on. From the sound, he knew that his den had been entered and a robbery was in progress. Mr. Rogers remained perfectly silent.

He could hear two voices. In the total darkness, he grabbed a pad and pencil and began to write down the conversation. For ten minutes, Mr. Rogers leaned against the door listening to the voices. Suddenly, all was quiet.

After a brief time, Mr. Rogers carefully opened the door and entered the den. A window was open. The robbers had used it to make good their escape. Mr. Rogers surveyed the room. All was in order except the bottom drawer of his desk, which had been locked. In it he kept a substantial amount of money and some jewelry. He found the drawer pulled open and completely empty.

Mr. Rogers estimates that $2,500 in cash and jewelry was stolen by the robbers. He would like the insurance company to pay him this amount so that he can replace his valuables.

After the robbery, the plaintiff immediately telephoned the police. EXHIBIT A is a photograph of the room taken shortly after the police arrived.

EXHIBIT B is the note written by Mr. Rogers as he listened at the door when the robbery was in progress. On it, he has written down some of the robbers' conversation. The names they called themselves are noted.

While the information Mr. Rogers had written down was scant, it provided police with sufficient details to search their files. The records of two criminals whose first names matched the ones Mr. Rogers had written down, and who were known accomplices are shown in EXHIBIT C.

Despite a search of their last known residence, police found no evidence that these men had been in the city at the time of the robbery.

Bowen Insurance company refuses to pay the $2,500 which Mr. Rogers has requested. The company insists there is weak evidence that a robbery took place. Instead, it charges that the plaintiff staged the theft. An investigator for the insurance company has explained to the court why his company refuses to pay the insurance claim. I quote from his statement:

"Mr. Rogers has reported two other robberies in the last three years. In each case there was no forcible entry. There were no clues to the theft, and the robberies remain unsolved.

"From the condition of the room following this present robbery, the police again found no evidence of forcible entry. You will note that the bottom drawer was not forcibly opened, despite the fact that Mr. Rogers has stated the drawer was always locked. This means that the robbers, if there truly were robbers, had to skillfully pick the lock to open the drawer.

"Since Mr. Rogers admits the robbers entered and left in a matter of ten minutes, we find his entire testimony highly suspect. Would intruders have entered the den without searching the rest of the house for valuables? Why did they limit themselves to the den? How did they know there were valuables in the bottom drawer? The relatively small amount stolen would not suggest a professional thief. We are asked to believe that two amateurs entered the house, picked the desk drawer lock, and escaped. All in a matter of ten minutes!

"In view of the plaintiff's previous reported thefts and the questions we raise about the present theft, my company refuses to pay the claim."

LADIES AND GENTLEMEN OF THE JURY: You have just heard the Case of the Speedy Jewel Thieves. You must decide the merit of Mr. Rogers' claim. Be sure to carefully examine the evidence in EXHIBITS A, B, and C.

Was a robbery committed? Or did Mr. Rogers stage the theft in order to collect the insurance money?

EXHIBIT A

Can you open the drawer?

Watch the lamp, Dave.

Hurry, I hear voices.

Look at this, Barry.

EXHIBIT C

RESIDENT KNOWN CRIMINAL

NAME Barry Waters

WHERE BORN USA

SEX M AGE 38 EYES Blue

HAIR Black HEIGHT 6'3" WEIGHT 216

DISTINCTIVE MARKS AND SCARS Scar above right eye

CRIMINAL SPECIALTY Breaking and entering

NAMES OF ASSOCIATES Dave Simpson

RESIDENT KNOWN CRIMINAL

NAME Dave Simpson

WHERE BORN USA

SEX M AGE 44 EYES Green

HAIR Brown HEIGHT 5'9" WEIGHT 150

DISTINCTIVE MARKS AND SCARS Missing finger, left hand

CRIMINAL SPECIALTY Breaking and entering

NAMES OF ASSOCIATES Barry Waters

VERDICT

THE ROBBERY WAS A FAKE.

Rogers said that he wrote down the conversation when his bedroom was in total darkness. But the words in EXHIBIT B are evenly spaced and are written in a straight line. Every *i* is precisely dotted and every *t* precisely crossed. This would have been impossible to do in a dark room.

Earl Rogers had faked the robbery.

The Case of
the Crazy Parrot

Ladies AND GENTLEMEN OF THE JURY:
When a store gives a warranty to its customers,
the store must fully stand behind that warranty.

The case you are asked to decide today involves
a pet shop. Mrs. Violet Hoffman, the plaintiff,
says that the parrot she bought at King's Pet
Shop has not lived up to the pet store's warranty.
Mr. Tom King, the defendant, disagrees.

Mrs. Hoffman has given the following testimony:

"It was my son Billy's birthday. He's such a
good boy, such an intelligent boy, such a creative
and curious child, that I wanted to give him an
unusual gift. I decided to buy him a pet parrot. I
visited several shops before choosing what I
thought was the perfect bird. My greatest concern
was that I find a parrot that was well behaved."

Tom King, the owner of King's Pet Shop,
assured Mrs. Hoffman he had exactly the bird
she was looking for. He had trained the parrot
himself. Mrs. Hoffman bought the parrot and
gave it to her son on his birthday.

Billy named the parrot Long John Silver. Long John quickly became a member of the Hoffman family. It spoke out at the most unexpected times and became the center of attention.

One Saturday afternoon, Mrs. Hoffman returned home from the hairdresser. Billy met her at the door with a pained look on his face. When Mrs. Hoffman entered the house, she was horrified to find the living room in disarray. Sofa pillows were strewn on the floor. Books had toppled from the shelves. A large vase had fallen off a table and was lying cracked on the floor.

Long John Silver was sitting quietly, perched on his pedestal.

In tears, Billy told his mother that the parrot had gone berserk. Billy explained that while his mother had been gone, he had been doing his homework. He was typing a school paper when Long John Silver became excited, talking and squawking loudly.

As Billy finished his paper, Long John's squawking suddenly stopped. The parrot jumped off the perch and proceeded to fly wildly around the room. It spread its wings, knocking over everything in reach. When the parrot hit the vase, the crashing sound seemed to make it even crazier. It continued to fly around the room, grabbing pillows in its beak and dropping them as it flew from one place to another.

Billy finally caught the bird and managed to

fasten it to the perch.

Mrs. Hoffman claims that the parrot's behavior violates the pet store's warranty. She not only wants to return the bird but demands payment for the broken vase, which she says was worth $3,000.

EXHIBIT A is the store owner's warranty, found on the bill of sale.

EXHIBIT B is a photograph of the living room where the damage took place. You will note the entire room is in a state of disarray. Fortunately, the only permanent damage was to the vase.

Mr. Tom King, the pet store owner, represents himself as a professional animal trainer with fourteen years' experience. His sworn testimony states:

"I have personally trained hundreds of animals — including dozens of parrots. Remember the movie *The Purple Pirate?* I trained the parrots for all the pirates in that picture. No animal trained by me as a household pet has ever misbehaved in the manner claimed here today."

Mr. King feels strongly about his professional expertise and states the parrot could *not* have done the damage. He believes the damage was caused by someone else, perhaps Billy, and that Billy's story is a cover-up.

Mr. King's attorney has submitted EXHIBIT C as proof of this assertion. It is a blow-up of a section of the photograph in EXHIBIT B. It draws your attention to a boomerang that is lying on a shelf in the room. Mr. King believes the vase could have been easily knocked over by this toy. He states that such a toy does not belong in a living room.

Mr. King suggests that during Mrs. Hoffman's absence, Billy may have been playing with the boomerang and accidentally hit the vase. The other damage was done to cover up the accident and direct blame at the parrot.

Mr. King is willing to take back the parrot. But he flatly refuses to pay for the broken vase, as a matter of principle. His professional reputation has been challenged, and he does not believe that the parrot, which he personally trained, was the cause of the accident.

LADIES AND GENTLEMEN OF THE JURY: You have just heard the Case of the Crazy Parrot. You must decide the merit of Mrs. Hoffman's claim. Be sure to carefully examine the evidence in EXHIBITS A, B, and C.

Should King's Pet Shop pay for the damage? Or is someone else responsible for the damage, possibly Billy Hoffman?

KING'S PET SHOP
TRAINING WARRANTY

King's Pet Shop warrants that birds trained by the store shall act in accordance with the behavior and in such manner as normally expected of birds who have undergone such training.

EXHIBIT C

VERDICT

KING'S PET SHOP
DOES NOT HAVE TO PAY.

Billy claimed he was typing his school paper when the parrot became agitated. Exhibit B shows the living room with his paper in the typewriter.

The typewriter case is nearby. With the case in this position it would have been impossible to move the carriage backward and forward. Billy broke the vase and put the paper in the typewriter to pretend he was doing schoolwork.

The Case of the Hunter's Shadow

LADIES AND GENTLEMEN OF THE JURY:
The difference between attempted murder and an accident may be as slight as the difference between breathing out and breathing in.

Please keep this in mind as you examine the case before you today. The State, represented by the district attorney, has accused John Goode of the attempted murder of Bradford Bedder. John Goode, the defendant, admits that he shot Bedder but says it was an accident.

John Goode has testified as follows:

"My name is John Goode. Two years ago, Bradford Bedder and I each invested $15,000 to build a sporting goods store on the outskirts of Walton City. The store's location is near a hunting preserve that attracts sportsmen from all over the county."

The men began with high hopes, calling the store Goode and Bedder Sporting Goods. On the day the store opened, each man bought the other a special hunting hat for good luck.

Despite good business when it opened, the store

soon ran into financial problems. A new discount store opened down the road and cut deeply into business. It sold the same kind of sports supplies as Goode and Bedder, but at much lower prices.

One day, John Goode decided to check the county files to see who owned the discount store. Much to his surprise, he found it was owned by his partner, Bradford Bedder. He concluded that Bedder was able to sell sports supplies for less at the discount store because the supplies had been secretly stolen from the Goode and Bedder warehouse.

John Goode was outraged! He immediately went to Bedder's home, only to learn that Bedder was camping with friends at the hunting preserve. Goode hurried to the campsite and saw Bedder standing outside a large tent.

Goode confronted Bedder with his findings and threatened him if he did not return the money he had made from the stolen supplies. Bedder simply laughed in his face, claiming that his partner could never prove he had stolen the supplies from the Goode and Bedder warehouse. John Goode, still angry, left the campsite.

Later that night, while Bradford Bedder was inside the tent playing cards with his friends, a rifle shot rang out. The shot pierced the side of the tent and Bedder fell down, a bullet lodged in his arm.

Gerald Pike, a fellow card player, darted outside

and ran after the intruder. He caught John Goode as he was running away, a rifle in his hand.

Police arrived and arrested Goode for the attempted murder of Bradford Bedder. But Goode claimed the shooting was an accident, and he had had no intention of harming Bedder. He said that he had decided their friendship was too important to lose over a business squabble, and he had decided to join the hunting party. As he was walking toward the front of the tent that night, the rifle fell out of his hand, hit the ground, and went off.

John Goode's attorneys have presented EXHIBIT A, which is a diagram of the tent where Bradford Bedder and his friends were playing cards when Bedder was shot. The spot is marked where John Goode was standing when he claimed he dropped his gun. Note that the tent flaps are closed, and there is no way Goode could have seen Bedder to purposely aim at him.

John Goode continues to claim that the shooting was an accident.

The district attorney called Gerald Pike to the witness stand. Mr. Pike testified that he had been in the tent earlier in the day and overheard John Goode threaten Bradford Bedder. EXHIBIT B presents Mr. Pike's testimony as he remembers the conversation. Goode was clearly angry and threatened Bedder, saying that if he did not pay back the money he stole, he would never live to spend it.

The district attorney has also presented EX-HIBIT C. He says it proves John Goode could have aimed at Bradford Bedder inside the tent even though the tent flaps were closed. He claims that Goode could have seen from the shadows on the outside wall of the tent, which man inside was his partner. Bedder and his friends were of similar height. But Goode could have identified Bedder if he somehow cast a shadow that was different than his friends.

The hats of Bedder and his two fellow hunters are shown in this exhibit. For demonstration purposes, the district attorney has placed a kerosene lantern similar to the one in the tent in front of the hats. A white background is behind them.

The district attorney has asked you to notice the similar shadows cast by two of the hats. But the shadow of the third hat, which is the special hunting hat Goode bought for Bedder, is very different. The district attorney has stated that Goode could easily have recognized the shadow of Bedder's hat, and he could have easily aimed at him and fired. Thus, the State claims, it *was* attempted murder.

LADIES AND GENTLEMEN OF THE JURY: You have just heard the Case of the Hunter's Shadow. You must decide the merits of the State's accusation. Be sure to carefully examine the evidence in EXHIBITS A, B, and C.

Was the shooting accidental? Or is John Goode guilty of attempted murder?

EXHIBIT A

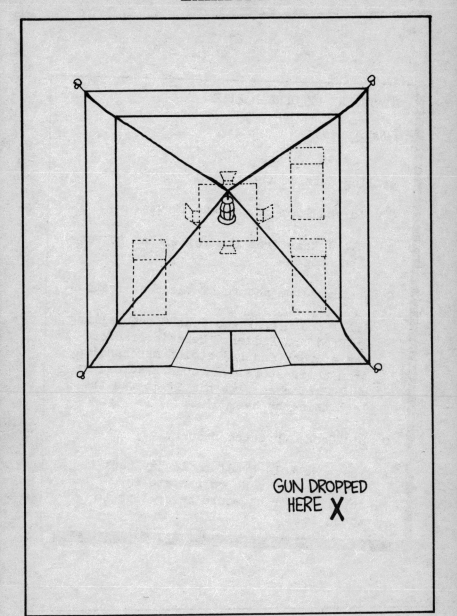

GUN DROPPED
HERE **X**

STATEMENT OF GERALD PIKE

(Continued)

yelling outside the tent.

Q   Did you look to see who it was?

A   No. I knew from the voice that it was John Goode.

Q   What was the nature of the conversation?

A   All I could hear was John Goode yelling at Bradford Bedder. He said Bradford was a crook and had stolen merchandise from their store. He told Bradford he would get even with him if it was the last thing he ever did.

Q   Did Goode threaten Bedder?

A   Yes. He told Bradford to pay back the money he had made on the stolen supplies, or he would never live to spend it.

EXHIBIT C

VERDICT

THE SHOOTING
WAS AN ACCIDENT.

In EXHIBIT A, the diagram of the tent, a kerosene lamp hanging from the ceiling is the only source of light. A light from above would have *cast all shadows on the floor*. From outside the tent, John Goode had no way of knowing where Bradford Bedder was sitting. Goode's story of the accidental firing was true.